Aesop's Fables

The Boy who Cried Wolf

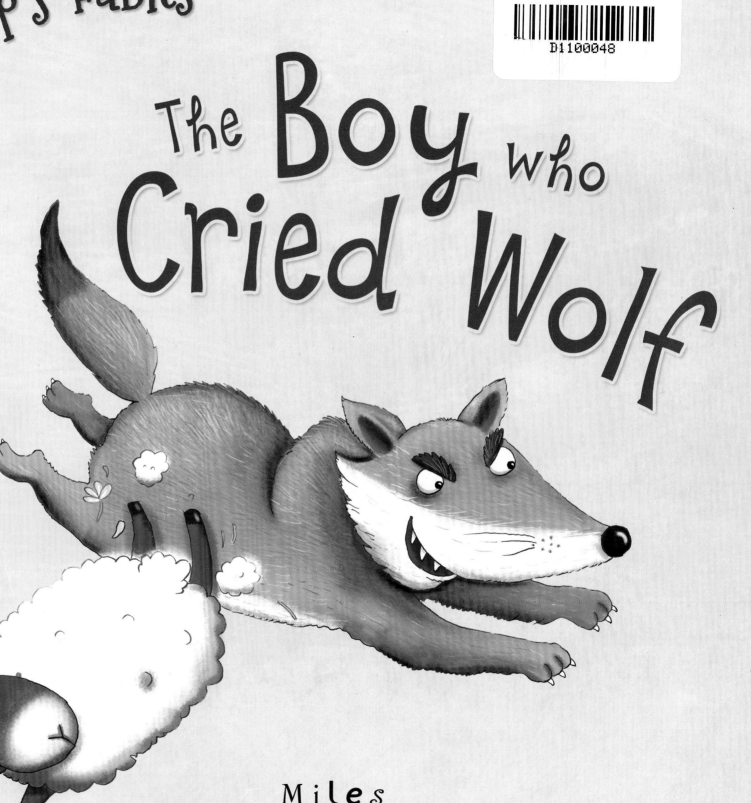

Miles Kelly

There was once a shepherd boy called George, who tended his sheep on the hilly slopes just outside of his town.

Baa baa!

Baa baa!

He worked all day by himself and often got lonely and bored with just his flock for company.

George tried to find ways to keep himself busy.

He got the sheep to jump over a stile, and counted them one by one, but this just made him sleepy.

He even gave them funny hairstyles. But the sheep weren't impressed.

Each morning George would move the sheep from field to field so that they could graze on the green grass.

But it was boring to watch them eat all day long.

He was fed up of having to rescue the silly sheep from hedges and ditches.

So one day, after spending all
morning trying to catch a naughty ewe,
George came up with an idea.

He left his flock
unattended and rushed
down the slopes towards
the town as fast as his
legs could carry him.

The townspeople jumped up and ran with George back to his flock.

They soon realized, however, that there was no wolf and returned to the town, grumbling.

George went back
to his duties for
the next few days,
but the weather
was cold and wet.

He didn't enjoy being out in the
rain at all, and started to think
about trying his trick again.

So the next morning he ran to the town again, shouting,

"Wolf! Wolf! There really is a wolf this time!"

He burst into the courtroom and ran up to the judge.

"You must come
and help me rescue
the sheep, otherwise
I will lose my flock!"

Again the townspeople came rushing to help him. But when they saw there was no wolf, just like the first time, they were very cross.

Soon after they left George noticed something moving in the trees.

He thought it was his eyes playing tricks but then he saw a furry body, bright eyes and sharp teeth.

The wolf came rushing
towards the sheep!
They ran away as fast
as they could!

Grrrr!

George waved his arms and shouted at the wolf to leave – but it was no good!

So he turned and ran, crying "Wolf!" in earnest this time.

He rushed into the town calling for help, but no one would listen!

He ran to the butcher, who shook his head and said, "You've lied one too many times."

Then he ran to the baker,
but he shook his head and
sent him away.

Eventually George gave up and hurried back to his flock.

Some of the sheep were missing and the rest had **scattered far and wide.**

The wolf was fast asleep, looking fatter than before.

George shouted at the wolf to wake him and chased him away at last.

It took George all day
and all night to gather
the rest of his flock.

George had learnt that...

a liar will not be
believed, even when
he speaks the truth.